# GAIL GIBBONS

# MY SOCCER BOOK

HarperCollins*Publishers*

Printed in Singapore at Tien Wah Press.

http://www.harperchildrens.com

Library of Congress Cataloging-in-Publication Data
Gibbons, Gail.
My soccer book / by Gail Gibbons.
p. cm.
Summary: Briefly describes the equipment, terminology, rules, positions,
and plays of one of the world's most popular games.
ISBN 0-688-17138-9
1. Soccer Juvenile literature.  [1. Soccer.]
I. Title.  GV943.25.G53  2000
796.334—dc21  99-34514  CIP

4  5  6  7  8  9  10

❖

Soccer is fun, whether you are playing yourself or rooting for your favorite team.

SOCCER BALL

To play, you need a soccer ball . . .

GOAL

GOALKEEPER'S
SHIRT

SHORTS

LONG SOCKS,
which often cover
SHIN GUARDS

SOCCER SHOES
with SOFT SPIKES
called CLEATS

and sometimes a uniform.

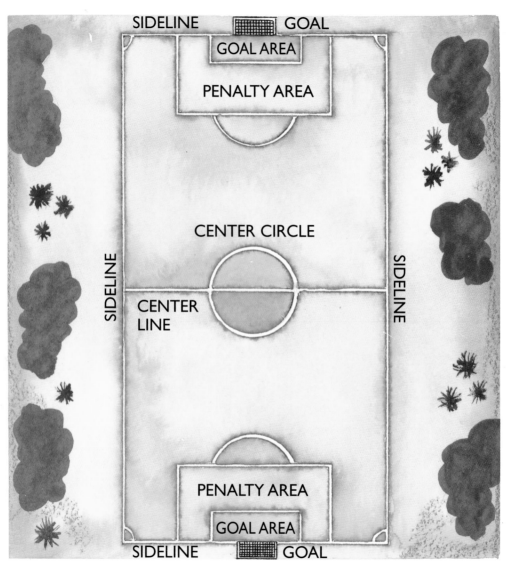

SIDELINE　GOAL

GOAL AREA

PENALTY AREA

SIDELINE

CENTER CIRCLE

CENTER
LINE

SIDELINE

PENALTY AREA

GOAL AREA

SIDELINE　GOAL

A soccer game is played on a soccer field.

The Honeybees

The Bear Cubs

There are usually eleven players on a team. These players work together, trying to score the most goals for their team. To score, the ball must go into the other team's goal.

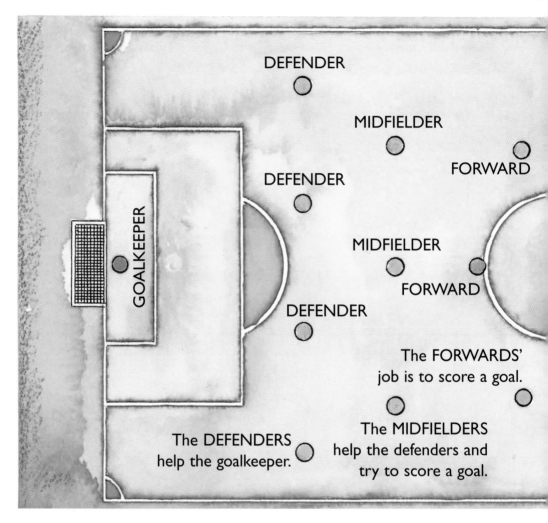

DEFENDER

MIDFIELDER

FORWARD

DEFENDER

GOALKEEPER

MIDFIELDER

FORWARD

DEFENDER

The FORWARDS' job is to score a goal.

The DEFENDERS help the goalkeeper.

The MIDFIELDERS help the defenders and try to score a goal.

Most of the time the players use their feet to control the ball. But any part of your body except your arms and hands can touch the ball.

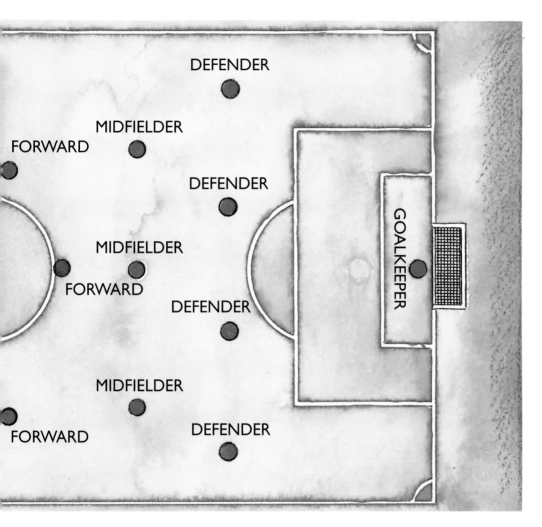

DEFENDER

MIDFIELDER

FORWARD

DEFENDER

MIDFIELDER

FORWARD

DEFENDER

GOALKEEPER

MIDFIELDER

FORWARD

DEFENDER

The goalkeeper, or goalie, tries to keep the ball from going into the goal. The goalie is the only player who can touch the ball with his or her hands or arms.

Games are often made up of two 45-minute halves.
Soccer games for kids are usually shorter.

The LINESMAN helps the referee make decisions.

The REFEREE makes sure the game is played fairly. He or she blows a whistle when a player commits a FOUL, or breaks a rule.

LINESMAN

To begin the game, the referee tosses a coin. Heads or tails? The team winning the toss has a choice—to kick the ball first or to select which side of the field to defend.

The team that gets the first kick is on offense. The other team is on defense. Let's play soccer! The ball is kicked from the center line toward the opposite team's goal.

Players on offense try to guide the ball closer to the other team's goal. Players on defense try to prevent the other team from scoring.

The ball flies into the goal. That's one point!

Now it's the other team's turn to kick off.

Players must follow a set of rules. You cannot push or trip another player, for instance. If you do, the referee blows a whistle.

You might be cautioned, or warned to behave, or you
might be sent off the field. The other team may be
allowed a free kick toward your goal.

Everyone gets a chance to kick the ball. It's exciting to make a great pass to a teammate or to score a goal.

The first half of the game is over. It's halftime, and the players catch their breath.

After halftime, the teams switch sides and go back into action. *Boom*—there's a great kick. But the goalie makes an even better stop.

The players run up and down the field as the ball goes back and forth.

There's just a minute left in the game. One last kick . . .

and it's a goal! The final score is two to one. Everyone cheers. It's been such a good game.

# MY SOCCER GLOSSARY

 **cleat**: a piece of rubber or metal attached to the bottom of a shoe for better traction

 **defense**: working to prevent goals, by blocking shots, stealing the ball, and other means

 **dribble**: moving the ball forward with your feet

 **foul**: doing something against the rules

 **goal**: the net or other space a ball must go into for a point to be scored

 **offense:** working to score goals, by taking shots, passing the ball, and other means

 **pass:** kicking the ball to a teammate

 **penalty kick**: After a major foul has been committed in the penalty area, the team that has been fouled chooses one player to take a kick at the goal. The goalie tries to prevent the penalty kick from going in, and all the other players stand aside.

 **sportsmanship**: playing fairly and enjoying a game, no matter who wins or loses

 **teamwork**: playing together as a team, encouraging and supporting all of your teammates